WALK IN MY GARDEN

WALK IN MY GARDEN

IF THEY HAD A VOICE

BRAD AYERS

Night Rain Books

Cover Illustration by Allyson Durkin

FIRST EDITION

Printed in the United States of America

ISBN 978-1-7348739-5-5

Night Rain Books / Night Rain Press

PO Box 445
Tillamook, OR 97141

Night.Rain.Press@gmail.com
http://NightRainBooks.com

CONTENTS

INTRODUCTION TO WALK IN MY GARDEN

Walking through the garden is a delightful experience full of surprise and wonderment at every turn. The plants, paths, fountains, sculptures, and garden art we discover are such amazing treasures. You also sense the love and care that has been given to make this garden a special place.

As you read the garden stories you will realize they have important things to say and teach us about life. Walk slowly, stop every now and then, look closely, listen carefully, feel gently, and let their bouquets work their magic. You now know they are talking just for you. But no matter what we try to write about the garden, nothing can say it better than a walk in the garden.

Let's start the walk, shall we?

1

WATERING CAN SPOUT OFF

JUST HOW MANY KINDS OF YOU ARE THERE?

When you are a garden watering can, you get this ridiculous no-answer question every time someone who doesn't know watering cans passes by. All you can do is show your stuff, if given the chance.

I know we can be confusing. Any assorted group of watering cans is overwhelming. We each have so many different handles, spouts, sizes, shapes, colors, and materials. We even come as elephants with trunks for spouts. How do you choose? Garden beginners are the most confused when selecting one of us. They have no idea how, or what, we can do. Or even what any of us are best at. Seems like trial and error is the only way they will learn. So, we watering cans just have to go through the agony with them until the learning is done. Who knows how long that will be?

But in the hands of an experienced and mature gardener we are a vital tool. We are essential to the garden's health. We can deliver just the right amount of liquid to the exact spot needed. We can even do this with liquid fertilizer diluted in water. A healthy watering can never fails to do its part when called into action.

One possible exception.

I used the word "healthy," you probably noticed. I did this on purpose. Even though we are such a good friend in the garden, we do sit or hang around most of the time. Because of this sitting around, we probably have a small amount of water left inside, or maybe some that is deposited by rain. Just enough water to encourage rust, especially during the winter. So, there might be a chance when you go to use me I have a hole some-where. And over the life span of a watering can, the vast majority of us develop a problem somewhere.

Kind of like you, to be frank about it.

I am not trying to make you upset. I'm just being realistic.

Fortunately, watering cans keep being produced and are avail-able in vast quantities at your garden supply store, online, or at garage sales. You might even inherit one, who knows. A rather unorganized journey to becoming your trusted garden watering can, but so be it. And like most things, the tried-and-true designs of the past are second-guessed and then redesigned by some smart young designer fresh out of college who never watered a garden.

Yes, I'm a little testy on this. I'm a watering can spout off.

2

TAKE MY PATH

Hey, over here!

My owners invited you to see their garden. My path can take you to see all the best parts and surprises. Come on, take those first few steps. Just trust me.

Now I have you. You will just have to see what I am talking about.

That's how it starts. I am your garden path. You are now smitten with a garden adventure to remember. I will take you to experience some wonderful things just around the next turn. The best paths like me never reveal their secrets at the start. We are just interesting enough to get you started. As you step down and around you are intrigued by my path construction under foot and what you come upon. You are amazed as it seems nature did its best. A good path seems like it has been there all along. Can you hear that water? Is it a stream, or a fountain? Somewhere up ahead, I think.

You and my path are one. We are meant for each other. It almost seems like we were designed by the same spirit. All your senses come alive. You just have to take it all in. But how? There is so much. Slow down then. Stop and sit a while on that old bench over there. Or even that log put right here on my path just for you, it seems. I know, you almost forgot to take pictures, didn't you? I see that camera hanging around your neck. When all your senses are being used you are so absorbed, nothing artificial even comes to mind. That is how I know my path is doing its job.

Are you rested now? I still have more to show you. I have saved the fountain and arbor for the crescendo of my garden path adventure. You now know why, as I already said, the best garden paths never reveal our secrets up front. That would spoil your experience. We like the anticipation and excitement of discovery.

You are not my only visitors. My owners walk me just about every day. And now you are here. Now and then other friends or neighbors stop by. And you know what? Every day is different. They all say so. Yes, just like you, my path is always changing.

You take my path yearning for the same things you saw last time. But all those are soon forgotten as you see what new has emerged even more amazing and wonderful. Both path and garden work their magic. How could it be so perfect?

Garden path, what's around your next turn?

3

MY FAITHFUL HOSE

ASIDE FROM THOSE DARN WEEDS, I can also be irritating.

Now don't get me wrong. A garden hose is essential to any garden. I'm your loyal and trusted friend. But we're just a little ornery most of the time. You would be too if you had to lay around outside in the elements.

Especially if you leave me filled with water under pressure. I could almost bust my gut.

Release the pressure next time!

Let's not get off on the wrong foot. I really do like my job in your garden. I like it best when you hold my nozzle in your hand and enjoy your watering. You are happy and I can see I am necessary. A few times each week I come to the rescue just in time to save some poor wilting flower. You are really kind to me when this happens. I get coiled neatly when we are done.

But on other occasions, like washing the car, or when you are in a hurry, we don't get along very well. Do you think I can just uncoil at a moment's notice? Sometimes it's cold and so am I. I need time to get going. You don't understand hoses. And you don't have much patience at these times either. So, I can really get your goat by kinking as you pull on me. The harder you pull the more I resist. This shuts down the water and you get so very upset. My snarls and tangles cause you to stop and waste some of your "so precious" time to straighten me out. You seem to resent that I have all the time in the world.

Another tense moment between us happens if I spring a leak. I probably didn't cause it but get the blame anyway. Looks like dog teeth marks to me. You should see how he treats me when you aren't home. Also, the kids really play rough and they seem to have this every day need in summer to jump through sprinklers or throw water balloons. And then there's that Slip-n-Slide thing that needs constant water running. But the cruelest of all is when you run over me in the driveway.

Hey, I'm not made for this kind of treatment. I'm only rated for so many hours.

Show a little sympathy for me. We can still be good friends. I just need a little understanding. Here are my suggestions. Take your time. Coil me up, not too tight. Put me in the shade. Pressure me down at the end of use. Wake me up slowly in the morning and keep the dog and kids away.

I'd rather water the garden with you.

4

TOMATOES TRY THEIR BEST

 MOST OF YOU PEOPLE GIVE UP ON us. You try a few times and quit saying, "I guess we just can't grow tomatoes here."

Sorry you feel that way. We really do try hard every season. Part of your problem is you have so many varieties to choose from. That may be your first critical decision. We come in most colors of the rainbow. Most think a tomato is red and we have plenty of those. But what about yellow, pink, and even purple with those heirloom varieties? And then other decisions like growing seasons cause you trouble. You often fall for the early ones when the best takes longer. Size and shape seem to baffle you too. Round, pumpkin or pear shape, small or large, and many more. I think your decision is based on some tomato experience from your childhood. The ones like grandma grew in her garden perhaps.

Have you made your selection yet? Ask for help then. Everybody has a tomato growing theory. Everyone seems to claim some level of success. This only makes you feel more and more like a tomato growing failure. OK—let's just make a choice and give me one more try. If this year is a disappointment you can plant flowers next year and forget tomatoes.

Here is what I can promise. Most of the time we will come so close. We flower, develop fruit, and grow a while. But then all kinds of things happen to spoil the happy ending. We get bottom rot, don't ever turn red, or just shrivel up. Horn worms love to munch on our leaves. Disease can get in to wreck things. Sometimes we don't do anything and just sit there. You eventually lose interest and stop watering. Amazing we still don't give up. We somehow keep a few green leaves and keep our branches and stock somewhat upright. Once in a while a miracle happens and we finally, unnoticed by you, produce a few ripe fruits.

But when the selection, season, and planting are just right, watch out. We can produce an amazing crop. So many you have to give them away. So many the neighbors say thanks, but we have plenty.

No more tomato failures for you. And when the opportunity arises, you gladly impart your tomato growing theory to anyone who asks.

Now you are the proud tomato growing experts.

Until next year.

5

GARDEN ART IS ANYTHING

"That's my garden art" you announce to visitors. Everyone stops, squints, and looks back again and sure enough, it is your garden art.

Well, I just happen to be one of those. I pose stately and proud in the garden ready for any visitor that comes by. Inevitably I get a slowdown, a pause, and a second look. The next thing are the comments. I can hardly keep a straight face as you go through the list. "What is it?" "What is it made out of?" "How clever." "Who made it?" I could keep going but I sense you are way ahead of me by now. You have seen your fair share. Nothing seems to escape being called garden art these days. Don't throw it away. Turn it around, rotate up or down, put on a little paint, add a few extras, and your new garden art is ready.

We belong to a large family of metals, woods, ceramics, glasses, bricks, stones, driftwood, and ropes. I apologize if I did not mention one of your favorites. Hard to keep up with the "any-thing goes" garden art trends these days. All I know is we try our best to reinvent ourselves every few years. And so far, it's working. Just when you say "I have seen it all" we pop up in new forms to amaze you.

Now for me, I am a relative old timer. I've been in the garden for, let's see, three or four years now. I am a combination of several natural and man-made materials. My main frame was salvaged one day from the "dump pile" by my owner who had an idea and a kind heart. I had sat around for several weeks but then, by chance, several more pieces turned up and were all rounded up. After considerable pushing, shoving, and twisting I was a foursome put together with some glue, screws, and wire.

Next came the decision where I should go in the garden. Now, this is where I have a gripe. I had no say in the matter. Why did I just have to fill in a hole in the foliage? I deserve a prominent spot, as do the prize plants. After all, I am more a part of the yard than some plant you just bought and stuck in the ground. But as it turned out, I was not consulted and ended partly hidden by some big leaf showoff. I ended up as a curiosity afterthought in my opinion.

No matter how bad this seems it could be worse. Remember the dump pile I almost didn't survive? I had some good friends there who were not as fortunate as me.

So, despite my complaining, I'm glad to be just another anything garden art you are so proud of.

6

MY FLOWER IS OPEN

Hey bee! Over here!

I just opened up this morning. I heard you buzzing yesterday and almost had a fit when you buzzed right by. You can't resist me now!

Such is the way of nature. Opportunity, persistence, and necessity all work for the common good. I get pollinated and you Mr. Bee, get some nourishment for the colony. Working together we survive and grow season after season. Oh yes, once in a while I get eaten a bit by insects or deer needing their food requirement. I don't really hold that against them. They are part of nature's plan too. So are the butterflies and hummingbirds who also visit me. But you bees are my favorite.

Sounds like a wonderful life for the flowers and bees, and it is. You humans should be as lucky. I hear far too much complaining. Stop and enjoy nature as it is rather than trying to control it. We will give you much more than you ever could dream of. It's fine to study us but why are new varieties constantly needed? Who said disease tolerant and fast growing were something to add? We were doing just fine. Yes, every now and then we have a rough time but so what? We are hardy. Just look at your research. We have been here a lot longer than you have. We must be doing something right.

Ok, I'll back off my soap box. After all, I just opened up this morning and put out my "open for business" sign. I am so happy to be a flower. I will enjoy the next few days with all my bee friends vying for my prime spot. And as they do, I will detect small amounts of my neighbor flower's pollen being left behind in my pedals. With my bee friends helping, I will do them a favor in return.

So, let's not get too upset when things don't go as planned. Your life and my flower bed require the same things. Water and nourishment, trimming for a little more elbow room, and a little weeding.

We need each other.

Treat me as you would a good friend.

I will give you smiles and good smells in return.

7

POT ME UP

I DESERVE MORE RESPECT FROM YOU IN-GROUND PLANTINGS.

I belong in the garden as much as you do. Sometimes I might just come off as stuck up or superior. You think I am too good for you ground guys? Do you think I am privileged or special? Perhaps my insecurity is showing.

Some say it's not a real garden if it's not in the ground. I'm a pot and I take offence to that attitude. Just because I am above ground with a special soil formula doesn't mean I can't grow plants. I even have some special capabilities. I can go places you ground guys can't like walks, decks, and patios. I can easily be moved around, and my plants oriented for best exposure as the sun path changes during the year. I can even grow stuff inside the house. You would never be invited there. But when you get right down to the basics, we can both excel using our unique features.

I'm not going to get into your business since this is supposed to be about pots. But I will confess right here, I can't do your job either. For example, I can't grow large things or produce big quantities efficiently. Glad we got that cleared up. Yes, I know I have done all the talking. This is my story, so I get the podium. I hope we can be friends anyway and stop arguing about who does the best job.

I admit, we each have our strengths and weaknesses. However, there are some things we can coordinate and help each other with. I can be a nursery for the young until they are old enough to be transplanted to your ground guys' garden. And you can produce clippings from mature plants for me to start new ones in my pots. Back and forth, we can handle plants as best suited for their growth stage. Kind of like the early childhood development they teach in those human schools. After all, we are dealing with plants that have defined growth stages. Seeds, sprouting, early growth, teen years, adult years, repair, and treatment in old age, and finally retirement.

See, we both serve needs. We both belong in the garden.

My pots and your ground.

I'm up and you're down.

8

HANG AROUND

LOOK UP. I'M UP HERE HANGING AROUND.

I get the best view and don't have to worry about all those ground slugs and pests. I get plenty of fresh air and sun. Ground plants think I am special. You do too. That's why you paid so much to buy me. And I do seem to get a lot of attention and admiring comments. I get put in the best places, hung on fancy brackets, and get most of your attention.

But hey, I'm just the same as those ground plants down there. I just happened to have been selected for the hanging basket. I really had no choice in the matter. But I'm not complaining. I can even put up with the other plants talking behind my back and knowing they are quietly smirking when they see me droop a bit in the afternoon heat. Or when you neglect grooming my dead flowers and I get to looking a little bit shabby.

Such is my life up here. Oh yes, almost forgot one more thing I have to put up with. Every once in a while, birds try to make me a nest. Most of the time it only lasts for a few days until my owner discourages any serious nest building. But, once in a while, we go to full nest, eggs, and all that chirping starts. At this point I really get special attention and careful watering. For some reason you suddenly get more caring and you start checking on me more often than normal. Three, four, five times a day! It drives me crazy.

But in the grand scheme of things my life as a hanging basket has a few good points. I am probably one of the most admired plants in the garden judged by the oohs and aahs I hear from you and the friends that drop by. You tell them all about me and how handsome I am. You add that I probably looked better last week but quickly add I am still holding on as the summer moves along. You add a touch of fertilizer with a little water and a sun rotation. Now I'm happy all the way to next week.

From another point of view hanging baskets are fairly high maintenance, or should I say, high attention. We have no ground reserves to draw from. We are exposed on all sides to drying wind and sun. We are often stranded in the air waiting for your attention. We regularly get a little dry and need a drink. We are waiting for you and your garden hose or watering can friends to come by, often just in time. You might consider a drip line next season to ease the stress on both of us.

And this is where I start dreaming. Yes, I know they say the grass is always greener. You ground plants want to be up here in the so-called prize location. You can have all the glory.

I just want to be down in the good old dirt.

Down where we are supposed to be.

9

THE OLD BIRD FEEDER

SIMPLY SAID, I AM A BIRD FEEDER.

I was placed in the garden to feed birds. That's all I do.

You may know that feeding birds dates back to early man. And since then, and over many centuries, it has expanded to a large commercial business and must-have garden accessories. What is a garden without at least one bird feeder?

But the story is just beginning.

Before we get too far it is only fair to give recognition to an important bird feeder that is not a part of this story. The hummingbird feeder is unique and must solve a number of challenges to properly nurture or our elegant and elite liquid-feeding bird friends. These delightful friends of the garden need specialized feeding fixtures and careful attention to feed formulation and hygiene to simulate the food sources they get in nature. Seed feeders do not.

As I said earlier, I am a bird feeder. I am home grown, and probably the simplest bird feeder (other than just throwing some seeds on the ground). I am a baking pan about 12 x 22 inches with low ½″ sides mounted on a five-foot plastic pole. I have drain holes drilled in each corner but otherwise I am just a plain baking pan. Nothing fancy. If you compared me to the bird feeders in today's catalogues and stores, I would be the ugly duckling. Everything else is high tech, bright colors, and engineered for specific bird types with all kinds of success claims.

Most gardens have had many bird feeders over the years including the garden I live in. Feeders come in all shapes and sizes. Even ones modeled after houses, cabins, barns, and almost any type of structure or container you can imagine. And today it is a serious international business industry with patents and advertising. The Bureau of Labor Statistics even has a beginner's course for this business. And Congress has even created a National Bird-Feeding Month. Must be big interest in the bird feeding business.

This brings up the point I am making that applies to just about everything.

I am not against innovation. The world could always use a better "mouse trap," or bird feeder in this case, if it actually worked, was more cost effective, and had no offsetting side effects. But therein is the catch. It never is all of these. My garden has seen many of these new models, as I said. No, I did not get offended when new ones arrived. I just watched. Some never attracted any birds. Others worked for a time but rusted away. Others were not very squirrel proof or easy to clean and restock. All these new, shiny, reengineered ones have come and gone and I'm still here, plain, sturdy, self-cleaning with rain, and well—just doing my job day after day.

Some would say my daily seed loading requirement is an unnecessary chore that the new "load-it-up" types solve. But others say this daily seed ritual is an important part. When you do it rain or shine it reinforces the reason you feed birds. You also get to see how birds of varying types interact and manage with my one-size-fits-all design. The feeding starts almost as soon as the birdseed is scattered on my tray. The Steller's Jays have scouts watching, seemingly knowing without a wristwatch when it is feeding time. They are the first to arrive, squawking loudly as they swoop down with excitement, followed by silent doves in pairs when in season. An occasional lone flicker may come by, and then a host of smaller birds in an array of colors and sizes. And, yes, a pesty small chipmunk on occasion. Somehow birds, all by themselves, have figured out a sequence and pecking order. No bird government to master plan it, or local bird police to enforce a bird-feeding law or regulation. Is it fair, you ask? Just don't change it, I say. The bird world is doing fine on its own with constant happy chirping. Every day, all the seeds are gone within three hours.

The purpose of a bird feeder is just that—to feed birds. And aside from all the obvious and well-studied benefits of birds in your yard as the reason to feed birds, you have the human emotional reward of doing something kind for your feathered friends.

The birds are good at finding food. They don't care if you feed them in a shiny new state-of-the art bird feeder, or in my old baking pan.

So then, why buy a new bird feeder? Go ahead, if it makes you happy.

The birds would say: spend that money for good birdseed.

AFTERWORD: IF THEY HAD A VOICE

Have you ever wondered what our world has to say?

We go about our lives midst all forms of non-human objects with only a passing thought, or no thought at all about them. And rarely have we even attempted a conversation.

What if we listen closely? What would they tell us? What could we learn?

You might be surprised at just how much they have to say about us.

This series of short stories started by an impromptu response to a prompt given in a writing class I took. The prompt was to write for 14 minutes on "something you keep." Out of the blue the image of a beach rock in my hand came to mind. Probably from one of many walks on the beach at Cape Meares, and even seeing others looking for that special rock. Or even seeing some- one's beach and shell collection neatly arranged or scattered around. We all have picked up a beach rock, held it a while, and maybe kept it to go home or dropped it for another. That day I wrote about this experience, completed the assignment, and filed it away with that hint of something undone.

Several months later as I was typing my handwritten responses to past writing prompts into the computer, I again read the story I had titled, "The Hopeful Beach Rock." I lingered a while, reading it again several times. And for some mysterious reason the stories started coming one after the other about other beach objects like driftwood, waves, the ocean breeze, and more. All had something to say about us. They even ask questions and heard our thoughts. They started our memories working and recalling earlier times, ones that were happy, sad, and adventurous.

After doing several beach stories I started to get images of other things we pass by, touch, or work with that should also get a chance to talk. Thus, started a much larger series of stories including things we sit on, doors we go through, and a range of others you will want to read about in the Voices collections.

This is the best part. I realized that in telling these as short stories, some call flash fiction, I could give you the chance to make it your own. I give each a range of emotions and experiences, but you will find it compelling to fill in and expand with your own.

As you read the stories remember only the non-human object does the talking. You have only to listen. The chair, for example, will ask you to remember what you were doing and thinking as you sat for a while, then suggests answers and asks even more questions. The door will recall memories of your emotions the door had observed as you passed through. Like a mirror, the door reflects these and suggests what you were thinking and whether you had any regrets. The beach rock wonders and asks you if you will keep it or discard it and choose another leaving you to determine the outcome. Interesting life lessons for sure.

Each reader of these stories will have a unique reaction to the observations and answers to the questions because all have different experiences. The one common link is we all have these kinds of memories. And each subsequent reading will only add to the recall and variations, with even new themes and outcomes of your own.

Some stories were written on the lighter side of things, playful, and happy times. Some are more serious with only hints of deeper concerns, but none are scary or tragic. Some have a moral bent and others suggest you read between the lines to get the nuance.

Most stories, however, are just plain fun.

ABOUT THE AUTHOR

I give most of the inspiration credit to the wonderful Northwest and Oregon coast. I arrived in 2015 and have not stopped creating in new and unusual ways. It inspires all art forms, and frankly just about anything you want to do. So, I give thanks for a second chance to prosper including my efforts of fiction writing and just recently song writing.

After a first degree in Fine Arts from California State University I went into business for my professional life. An MBA from the University of Denver followed while working for three major US companies, then running and starting my own along the way.

Concurrent to the business side I was an adjunct professor in the MBA program for the University of Phoenix for over 30 years.

I guess I was destined to return to the creative side of life, now at the ripe old age of 81. Old dogs, new tricks? Perhaps in this case. Yes, this is not your typical "about the author?" Blame the weather.

VOICES PUBLICATION COLLECTION

Beach Voices

The Chair Has Something To Say

Walk in My Garden

Doors We Walk Through

What's in The Box

Clothes Get Testy

Food Talks Back

ALSO BY BRAD AYERS

A Life's Journey

Beach Voices

Chair Voices

www.ingramcontent.com/pod-product-compliance
Lightning Source LLC
Chambersburg PA
CBHW070653130626
46555CB00006B/2852